MARC BROWN

ARTHUR'S BIRTHDAY

FOR: Arthur
FROM: Francine

SCHOLASTIC INC.

NEW YORK   TORONTO   LONDON   AUCKLAND   SYDNEY

FOR ALEX, SUNNY, AND KATE, THE BEST NEIGHBORS

ISBN 0-590-37759-0

12 11 10 9 8 7 6 5 4 3   9/9 0 1 2 3/0

Printed in the U.S.A   09

"I can't wait! I can't wait!" said Arthur.
"Are you sure it's only Tuesday?"
"See for yourself," said Mother.

"Four more days until my birthday!" said Arthur.
"I hope everyone can come to my birthday party."
"What kind of cake should I bake?" asked
Grandma Thora.

"Chocolate!" said Arthur.
"Have a good day at school," said Mother, smiling.
"And don't forget to hand out your invitations,"
said D.W.

"Buster, can you come to my party?" asked Arthur.
"Are you kidding?" said Buster. "Of course!"
"Grandma's making chocolate cake," said Arthur.
"I'll be there!" said the Brain. "I love chocolate."

"How about me?" asked Binky Barnes.
"You're invited," said Arthur, "and Francine, too."
"Oh, boy," said Francine, "we can play spin the bottle!"

"Muffy, can you come to my birthday party?"
Arthur asked.

"Sure," Muffy answered. "When is it?"

"Saturday afternoon," Arthur said. "I can't wait."

"This Saturday afternoon? But that's when I'm having my party!" said Muffy.

"Oh, no!" said Arthur. "You can't.

"Can't you change your party to another day?"

"Are you kidding?" said Muffy. "The rock band and Pickles the Clown have been booked for months."

"I can't change my party, either," said Arthur.

"All my relatives are coming from Ohio."

No one knew what to do.
Should they go to Arthur's
birthday party?

Or Muffy's?

Wednesday before school, the boys had a meeting.
"I think we should stick together," said Buster.
"Me, too!" said Binky.
"Right!" said the Brain. "We're all going to
Arthur's party."
"But what about the girls?" asked Arthur.
"Who needs girls?" said Buster.

The girls met out at the playground during lunch.
"Anyone who doesn't come to my party can't be my
friend," said Muffy.
"But it won't be as much fun without the boys,"
said Francine.
"Are you my friend or not?" asked Muffy.

Thursday after school, Arthur and his mother
picked out decorations for the party.
Later, the delivery man brought a big box.
"Wow! This weighs a ton!" said D.W.

In the mail, there were three birthday cards
for Arthur.
One was from Uncle Bud. When Arthur opened it,
three dollar bills fell out.
"Some people have all the luck!" said D.W.

On the way home from school Friday, Arthur ran to catch up with Francine.

"I wish you could come to my party," said Arthur.

"I promised Muffy," said Francine. "But I wish I could go to both. What's a party without boys?"

They ran to Arthur's tree house.
Arthur found pencils, paper, and envelopes.
"Let me write them," said Francine. "It has to look like Muffy's handwriting."
"Okay," said Arthur, "but be sure there's one for all the girls."

That night Arthur told his parents about his plan. Early the next morning, Arthur and Francine delivered their notes: one to Prunella, one to Sue Ellen, and one to Fern.

The last note they delivered was a special one.
"All done," said Arthur.
"See you later!" said Francine.

"I smell pancakes!" said Arthur when he got home.
"Your favorite," said Father.
"And maple syrup all the way from Ohio," said
Aunt Bonnie.
"Happy birthday!" said Cousin George.

"Time for birthday kisses," said Mother.
"And eight birthday hugs," said Grandma Thora.
"Don't forget a pinch to grow an inch!" said D.W.

Arthur stood by the window. It was almost noon.
"Someone's coming!" he cried.
It was Sue Ellen.

"What are you doing here?" asked Sue Ellen.
"What are you doing here?" asked Buster.
"It's a surprise for Muffy," said Francine, coming up behind them.
"It's a surprise for all of us!" said the Brain.
"Everyone find a place to hide," said Arthur.
"Muffy will be here any minute!"

"Shhhh!" whispered Buster. "Here she comes!"
Arthur opened the door.
"Hi, Arthur, I came to pick up my present,"
said Muffy.

"Surprise!" shouted everyone.

"Happy birthday, Muffy!" said Arthur.

"See I told you, your present is too big to carry."

"The rest of your party is on the way,"
said Francine.

"After all," said Arthur, "what's a birthday party
without all your friends!"

"This is the best birthday ever," said Muffy. "We should do this every year!"
"But next year at your house," said Arthur's mom.

"Time to open presents," said Francine. "I picked this one out especially for you. You have to promise me you'll use it right away."
"Sure," said Arthur. "I can't wait."

"Happy birthday, Arthur!"